WHO D

How
To Be a Detective
in Ten
Easy Lessons

Also by Marvin Miller:

YOU BE THE JURY
YOU BE THE JURY: COURTROOM II
YOU BE THE JURY: COURTROOM III
YOU BE THE JURY: COURTROOM IV
YOU BE THE DETECTIVE

WHO DUNNIT?

How
To Be a Detective
in Ten
Easy Lessons

Marvin Miller

Illustrated by Bob Roper

SCHOLASTIC INC.

New York   Toronto   London   Auckland   Sydney

These stories were previously published in **Games Junior Magazine**.

ISBN 0-590-44717-3

12 11 10 9 8 7 6 5 4 3 2 1   1 2 3 4 5 6/9

Printed in the U.S.A.   40

First Scholastic printing, November 1991

for Wendy and Gary

Detective Casefiles

Introduction

This book will tell you all about being a master detective. The information is TOP SECRET. Share it only with a friend you can trust.

A detective needs sharp powers of observation. Evidence he or she discovers comes in many forms. The puzzles in this book will show you how to search for clues and how to understand what they mean.

Sometimes a detective needs to send a message to a partner. Just look inside to find out about secret codes and hiding places.

You also will discover important detective tips. But be careful when you use them. They are closely guarded secrets!

And, finally, you will get a chance to do some mystery solving yourself. Ten picture mystery stories are in this book. You can follow along with Officer Fred Dumpty and put your detective skills into action. As you finish each casefile, turn to the Top Secret Solutions and see if your answers are on target.

I hope you have hours of fun with this book. So turn the page and get to work. You're on your way to becoming a master detective!

Marm Mille

DETECTIVE CASEFILE #1

The Case of the Soggy Suspect

Officer Fred Dumpty liked solving crimes almost as much as he liked to eat. In fact, if he didn't spend so much time thinking about eating, he surely would have been promoted to the rank of detective by now.

One night, a hungry Officer Dumpty turned the corner onto Valley Street, looking for an open doughnut shop, when a sudden rainstorm began. As he rolled up the window of his police car, he saw a woman waving to him frantically.

His thoughts turning from food to felony, he raced to the scene and found Mrs. Turner in tears.

"My purse! A man just stole my purse. He ran that way." Mrs. Turner pointed to a small street up ahead.

"Did you get a good look at him?" Dumpty asked.

Mrs. Turner held back sobs. "It happened so fast. He came up from behind me and grabbed my purse. When I turned around, all I could see was his back. I can't begin to describe him."

Dumpty stepped on the gas and sped through the rain in the direction Mrs. Turner had pointed. It was a long street lined on both sides with small shops. Dumpty parked his police car and carefully checked the stores one by one. All were closed, and their doors were securely locked.

A restaurant at the end of the street was brightly lit. His stomach rumbling, Officer Dumpty went inside, where the smell of the meat loaf special wafting from the kitchen made his mouth water. But, keeping his mind on the business of detection, he walked over to a waitress who was cleaning off a table.

"Did anyone come in here in the past ten minutes?" he asked.

"I don't know," she replied. "I've been in and out of the kitchen."

The restaurant was practically full. As Dumpty surveyed the room his eyes rested on two interesting things: One was a slice of delicious-looking apple pie under a glass lid. The other was a man sitting alone in a booth.

When Officer Dumpty walked toward him, the man put down his coffee cup and looked up from a paperback book he was reading. Quite casually, Dumpty asked, "How long have you been here?"

"Almost an hour," the man answered. "I heard you ask the waitress if she saw anyone come inside. But I can't help you either, Officer. I've been reading this terrific mystery book. It's so scary I can't put it down."

At that moment, Dumpty knew that he wouldn't have time for a bite to eat. Instead, he said to the man, "I'd like you to come with me to police headquarters concerning a stolen purse."

Examine the picture of Officer Dumpty speaking with the man in the booth. Why did Dumpty think he had caught the purse snatcher?

FILE ENTRY: Footprint Clues

Here are normal footprints of a person walking. Notice the direction the feet point, the distances between steps, and the firm impressions of the heels and toes. Now look at six sets of footprints that are a little more unusual. **Can you match each set (1–6) with one of the descriptions (A–F)?**

Descriptions

A. Pulling a wagon
B. Running
C. Very tall person walking

D. Pushing a wheelbarrow
E. Limping
F. Walking with a cane

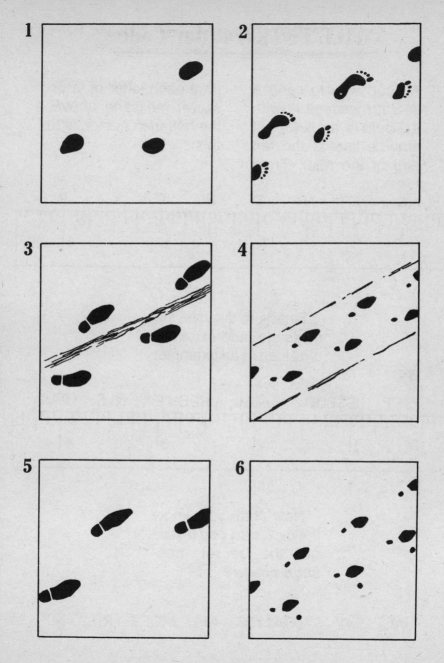

FILE ENTRY: Ruler Code

A good way to send a secret message is with the help of a ruler. First draw a line at the left end of the ruler. Then print each letter of your secret message above the half-inch marks, like this:

↓ S E N D H E L P

Finally, to disguise the message, add extra letters. Here's an example:

↓ RJST ESLUIN RADH LHEBUE NLS OPUR

Now that you know the trick, **can you figure out the secret message below?**

↓ I EWL SAY IOANTS AFL MOER RU TMF E

8

FILE ENTRY: Detective Tip

If you have a drawer where you keep secret things, here's a way to find out whether someone else has opened it.

With saliva, stick a hair across the crack in the drawer, as shown in the illustration:

If someone opens the drawer, the hair will become unstuck.

DETECTIVE CASEFILE #2

The Case of the Bald-Headed Suspect

"I came as fast as I could, Sergeant." Officer Fred Dumpty stood panting in the doorway to Sergeant Rider's office.

Dumpty had been called to the office in the middle of a quick bite, and powdered sugar from a doughnut coated the front of his uniform.

"Close the door, Dumpty, and clean off your uniform," said Rider gruffly, from behind his desk. "I've told you to pay more attention to your appearance."

Rider was furious, but Dumpty soon found out that it wasn't only because of Dumpty's uniform. In a low voice seething with anger, Rider said, "We managed to capture Bart Hargrove and we brought him here until federal officers arrive."

"That's great!" cried Dumpty. "He's wanted in four states. The mayor will give you a commendation."

"No, you idiot, he'll probably fire me. Hargrove has just escaped. It'll cost me my badge."

Though the sergeant often criticized Dumpty, he wasn't a bad guy and he needed Dumpty's help. "Do we have any clues?" asked Dumpty.

"We have a report that a man fitting Hargrove's description stole a motor scooter and headed east not more than twenty minutes ago."

"He can't get very far," said Dumpty. "If he's headed east, I can overtake him. But what does he look like?"

Sergeant Rider handed him a wanted poster. "Too bad this isn't a clear picture. But since Hargrove is as bald as a honeydew melon and is wearing prison clothes, he should be easy to recognize."

Rider groaned. "Not anymore. He stole an officer's street clothes from his locker, then shoplifted another outfit from a clothing store. We don't know what he's wearing now."

"Sounds bad, but I'm glad you have confidence in me to find him, Sarge."

"Don't call me Sarge," barked Rider, who did everything by the book. "And by the way, you're not finding anybody, I am — you're driving me."

In the police car, Dumpty told Rider that the motor scooter couldn't have traveled more than ten miles. "The farthest he could have got is Dover City." Minutes later, they arrived at the outskirts of town. As he passed Walden's General Store, Dumpty put on the brakes. There was a motor scooter in the parking lot.

"Wait in the car while I check out the store," said Rider. "Maybe Hargrove stopped to buy food."

"Say, Sergeant, could you buy me a bag of potato

chips while you're in there? I haven't eaten lunch yet."

"Do you ever stop thinking about food, Dumpty? Buy it yourself."

Dumpty happily followed Rider into the store. Inside, Rider spotted a suspicious-looking man at the checkout counter. He was wearing a big hat pulled down tight over his head. He seemed to fit the description of Hargrove. "Dumpty," whispered Rider triumphantly, from behind a display rack, "he must be Hargrove. He put on a hat to cover his bald head — why else would he be wearing a hat inside the store? I'm going to arrest him." He started to pull out his revolver.

"Buutsaarg . . ."

"What did you say, Dumpty?"

Behind him, Dumpty swallowed the potato chips he had been eating. (He was going to pay for them at the counter.) "But, Sarge, I think you're making a big mistake."

Rider's face turned red. "Who cares what you think? Look at you, potato chips all over your uniform. A cop who doesn't pay attention to appearances isn't much of a cop."

Dumpty simply smiled and whispered something into Rider's ear. "As much as I hate to admit it, I guess you're right, Dumpty. He's not our man. Let's continue into town before Bart Hargrove gets much farther."

Examine the picture of Officer Dumpty and Sergeant Rider inside the general store. How did Dumpty know the man wasn't Bart Hargrove?

FILE ENTRY: Lip Reading

Some detectives read lips to learn valuable information. While on a stakeout, a detective saw several suspicious-looking persons enter a guarded door. Each was allowed inside by using a secret password that changed daily.

To the right is what the detective saw through her telescope during the six days of her stakeout. She took a picture of the person's lips just as the person was starting to pronounce the secret password.

Can you match the pictures (1–6) with the following passwords (A–F)?

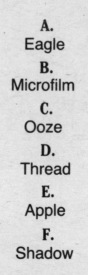

A.
Eagle

B.
Microfilm

C.
Ooze

D.
Thread

E.
Apple

F.
Shadow

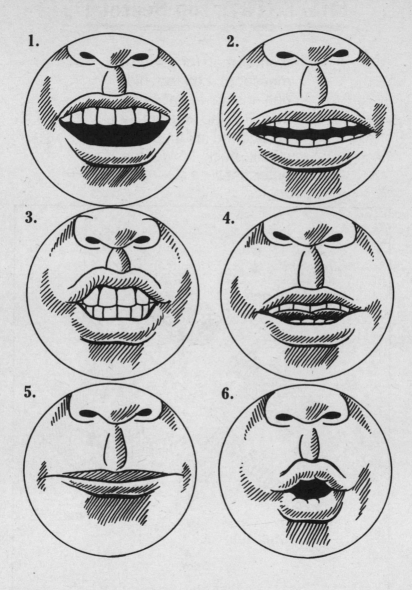

FILE ENTRY: Top Secret Tip

A small map (or a secret message) can be hidden inside a ball-point pen. Roll the map tightly around the ink tube and slip it back inside the outer shell.

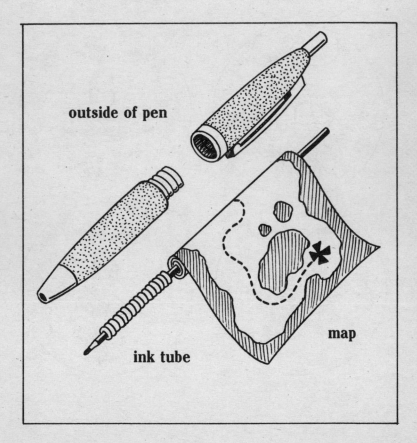

outside of pen

ink tube

map

FILE ENTRY: Mystery Riddle

Officers Davis and Horton were searching for a stolen box of rare coins that was hidden in a trash dump. They came to an abandoned sewer pipe, just large enough for one of them to squeeze through. Davis went through one end and Horton went through the other. Each crawled through the entire pipe and came out the other end. **How?**

DETECTIVE CASEFILE #3

The Case of the Snowball Slinger

Officer Dumpty stamped snow off his shoes as he opened the front door of Washington School. Mr. Woodward had been the principal when Fred Dumpty attended Washington as a kid — and he was still the principal. Though grown-up, Dumpty was nervous at the thought of having to see Mr. Woodward.

Inside, Mr. Woodward frowned at Dumpty and said, "You're not very prompt, Fredrick." Dumpty winced: He hated being called Fredrick. "Sorry, Mr. Woodward."

The principal pointed down the hallway. "Vandalism, Dumpty! Someone threw a snowball through Mrs. Gilbert's window."

The two men entered the classroom. Dumpty carefully examined the broken glass lying on the floor. Nearby, a puddle was all that was left of the snowball.

"What time did this happen, Mr. Woodward?" asked Dumpty, somewhat shyly. It felt peculiar to be questioning his former principal.

"About an hour after school let out," Mr. Woodward replied gruffly. "I'd guess about four-thirty." Being interrogated by a former pupil was annoying.

"Any idea who did it?"

"It must have been someone in Mrs. Gilbert's class. It could have been Tommy Hummer. He's a troublemaker. In fact, I punished him for throwing snowballs at some children during lunch recess."

Officer Dumpty got Tommy's address from the school files and drove to the Hummer house. He disliked solving cases at dinnertime. It was difficult for Dumpty to concentrate when he was hungry, which was often.

When he rang the bell, Mrs. Hummer opened the door. Fred Dumpty introduced himself and stepped inside. He saw Tommy peering from behind his mother's back.

Dumpty described to her the act of vandalism and

the fact that Tommy had been punished for throwing snowballs. Mrs. Hummer smiled warmly and said, "He was probably just having some fun. Didn't you ever throw snowballs at kids when you were his age?"

Dumpty said yes, and at the same time became aware of the delightful smell of a roast cooking in the oven. Mrs. Hummer noticed this and invited him to stay for dinner. "Thanks for the offer, but right now I have to ask a few more questions. Where was Tommy at four-thirty this afternoon?"

"He was right here in this house, playing video games all afternoon," she replied, still smiling pleasantly.

"How can you be sure?"

"I get home from work at four o'clock every day. Today, Tommy was already home when I arrived. But enough questions, let's get ready for a delicious meal."

Dumpty glanced at Tommy, who had moved closer to his mother. "One last one. Did he leave the house at all?"

"No," said Mrs. Hummer, the smile gone, her voice beginning to rise. "I told you he was here all afternoon! He came home right after classes."

"Well then," said Dumpty, "you'd both better come with me to the school. Tommy wasn't playing his video games all afternoon. He was outside when you came home."

Officer Dumpty continued. "You're covering up for him, so he must have been the one who threw the snowball. But I won't charge Tommy with mischief. It's up to the principal to figure out his punishment."

"You can forget about dinner, then," said Mrs. Hummer in a huff.

Dumpty nodded sadly.

Examine the picture on the following page of Officer Dumpty speaking with Mrs. Hummer. Why did he think she was lying??

FILE ENTRY: Detective Tip

If you want to walk up a flight of creaky stairs without making any noise, follow these directions. First, take off your shoes. Then, walk on the outside tip of the steps. The stairs will squeak the least that way.

FILE ENTRY: Secret Graph Code

You can use ordinary graph paper to send a secret message to a friend. First, cut a strip from the graph paper and print letters of the alphabet in twenty-six of the boxes. Your alphabet strip should look like this:

| A | B | C | D | E | F | G | H | I | J | K | L | M | N | O | P | Q | R | S | T | U | V | W | X | Y | Z |

To create the secret message, lay the alphabet strip below the first row of boxes on a blank piece of graph paper. Draw a star or an X in the box above the first letter in your message. Then slide the alphabet strip below the second row, and draw a star in the box above the second letter of your message.

Continue this way until your message is complete. For example, here is how to encode the message "BEWARE":

It may take too much graph paper to send a long message this way. But by using numbers instead of stars, you can reuse the same rows for different parts of your message. Instead of drawing a star in each box, write the number 1. When you get to the bottom of the piece of graph paper, go back to the top and continue your message, this time writing the number 2 in each box. If you get to the bottom again, continue at the top with the number 3, and so on. (Sometimes you may have to place more than one number in a box.)

If you like, you can also skip a row of boxes between words. That's been done in the following message. **Can you decipher what it says?**

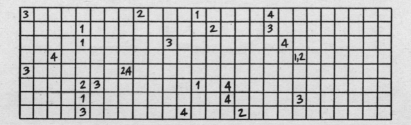

FILE ENTRY: Mystery Riddle

When Henry joined the Glendale police force, his picture was on the front page of the town's weekly newspaper. Everyone thought he would help make the town safer. As time went by, Henry worked on many of Glendale's toughest cases, and was highly praised. But he never received a promotion. In fact, Henry was never even paid for his work on the police force. **Why?**

DETECTIVE CASEFILE #4

The Case of the Lost Locomotive

When Officer Fred Dumpty entered Bell's Hobby Shop, Mr. Bell was leaning against the counter, head in hands, as if he were in pain.

Looking up, he said in a voice that cracked, "Nancy Gibson. She must have stolen the Silver Arrow. And to think I trusted her."

The Silver Arrow was the most expensive model locomotive in the store — a collector's item that worked better than some real-life Amtrak engines.

Mr. Bell pointed to the display shelf, where a line of passenger cars sat on the tracks. The engine was missing.

Dumpty scratched his head and took out his notepad, musing to himself. How come the sergeant sends Mallory to investigate bank robberies, and I get stolen choo-choo trains? But then he thought: No case was too small for a great detective like Sherlock Holmes to solve, and no case is too small for Officer Dumpty! Speaking aloud, Dumpty said, "What makes you think it was the Gibson girl?"

The owner hesitated, as if he didn't really want to get Nancy in trouble. "Nancy loves collecting things — toy soldiers, thimbles, wind-up toys. And especially model trains. She always stops here after school and plays with the Silver Arrow. She wanted to buy it, but she said it would take a long time to save up for it on her allowance."

"When do you think it was stolen?" Dumpty asked Mr. Bell.

"It couldn't have been more than a half an hour ago," Mr. Bell replied. "Around eight-thirty. I was closing my store for the night and went into the back room. When I returned, the train was gone. That's when I phoned the police."

It was a long, hot drive to the Gibson home. Dumpty rolled down the window to cool off. To save gas money, the sarge told his men to turn off their air-conditioning. Well, Sherlock Holmes didn't have air-conditioning at 221B Baker Street, either. When a sweaty Dumpty arrived, he rang the bell several times. No one answered. Dumpty decided to wait.

After fifteen minutes, Officer Dumpty knocked as

loudly as he could. A minute or two later, Nancy Gibson opened the door.

"Where have you been?" Dumpty asked sharply. The heat was making him irritable.

"I was reading *Antique Model Railroad* magazine in my clubhouse in the backyard. I built the clubhouse to keep all the things I collect. It's much cooler in there. With the door open, there's a nice breeze."

Officer Dumpty gave the girl his sternest look, one he had practiced in front of the mirror. "Someone stole the Silver Arrow from Bell's. Do you know anything about it?"

Nancy Gibson stared at him, eyes wide with innocence. "Gee, Officer, it wasn't me. Take a look in my clubhouse — I'll even let you in without a search warrant."

They walked to the backyard and opened the clubhouse door. The room was pitch-black. Nancy lit the candle on the table.

"If you were reading in here," said Dumpty, "how come the candle is out?" Gotcha, thought the officer.

Said Nancy coolly, "I blew it out when I went to see who was knocking."

Darn, thought Dumpty, she's quick. The officer scanned the room, filled with thimbles and toys and wind-up toys and model railroad trains. But no Silver Arrow. Nancy shrugged her shoulders.

Sherlock would never have been outwitted by a thirteen-year-old, thought Dumpty, desperately. He looked at the room again and this time he had an idea. He turned to Nancy:

"You're sure you were here tonight?"

She nodded with a smile.

"Well," said Dumpty, "I know for a fact you weren't in your clubhouse when I rang your doorbell. At that moment, I suspect you were still returning from Bell's Hobby Shop, and I'll bet you had the Silver Arrow with you. You must have used the back door so that I wouldn't see you arrive."

"How do you know that?" asked Nancy.

"Elementary," replied the officer.

Examine the picture of Officer Dumpty speaking with Nancy Gibson. Why did he think she was lying?

FILE ENTRY: Spotting Spots

Detectives can discover clues by studying spots. Here are different marks left by a person eating a chocolate ice-cream cone. The marks were made by the dripping ice cream.

Can you match the drops (1–6) with the descriptions of the person eating the cone (A–F)?

A. Standing on the ground

B. Sitting on top of a ladder

C. Standing in the same place for several minutes

D. Walking toward your right

E. Walking toward your left

F. Standing on a balcony above a wall

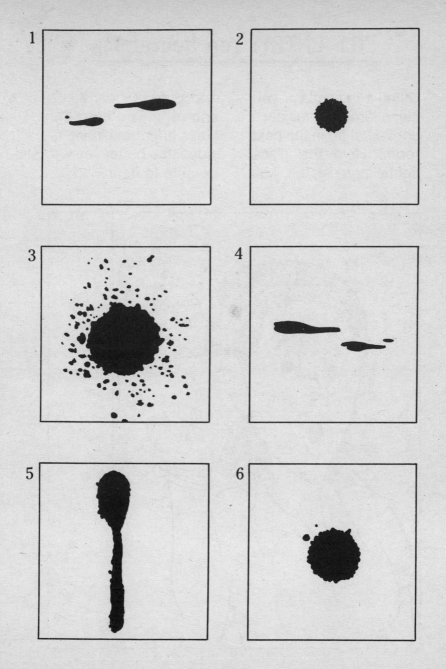

FILE ENTRY: Top Secret Tip

Using a water glass, you can overhear a subject's conversation in the next room. Hold the glass tightly against the wall and put your ear to its open end. The larger the glass and the thinner its sides, the better you will be able to hear.

FILE ENTRY: Mystery Riddle

Two police officers hid behind a hedge to watch for speeders they could give tickets to. One officer looked up the road and the other looked down it, so as to cover both directions.

"Ann," said one, without turning his head, "what are you smiling at?"

How could he tell that Ann was smiling?

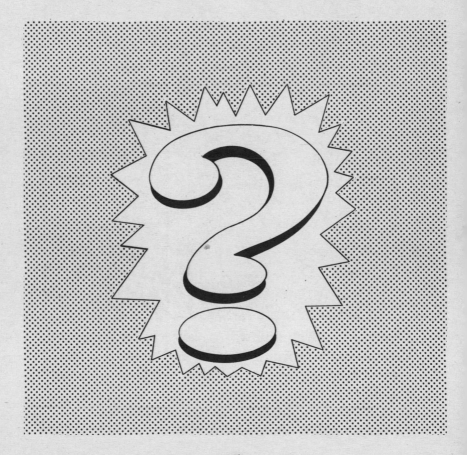

DETECTIVE CASEFILE #5

The Case of the Darling Dog

Officer Fred Dumpty was barely awake. It was the start of his morning rounds, and he lazily cruised down Greenleaf Street, on the outskirts of town, enjoying the peace and quiet.

"Help! Police! Murder!" he heard suddenly.

Dumpty nearly jumped out of his seat. Across the

street, a woman holding a little dog was screaming hysterically. Dumpty pulled his car over to find out what had happened.

"My little Terrie has been brutally attacked by Billy Harris," wailed Mrs. Smithers. "I demand you arrest that hooligan and throw him in jail."

"Is Terrie your daughter?" asked Dumpty urgently. "Shall I call an ambulance?"

"No, you fool, Terrie is my sweet darling dog. Can't you see the awful lump on the head she got from that stone?"

Indeed, there was a small lump on the top of the dog's head. Slightly annoyed by Mrs. Smithers's tone of voice, Dumpty said, "She'll be fine. Now tell me what happened."

"It's that newspaper boy, Billy Harris," said Mrs. Smithers, placing Terrie on the ground. Instantly, the dog started growling at Dumpty.

"Why don't you start at the beginning," said Dumpty, nervously watching the dog.

"It was eight o'clock this morning and I had just let Terrie outside. A few minutes later I heard something hit my front door. And then my Terrie let out a big howl."

Dumpty walked over to the door to look at the two large stones in front of it, one of which had hit Terrie. As he did so, Terrie raced up and clamped her jaws on Dumpty's leg. Dumpty tried to shake her off.

"Police brutality!" yelled Mrs. Smithers.

"Get her off me or I'll give her a ride to the dog pound."

After Mrs. Smithers retrieved her dog, Dumpty tried to calm her down.

37

"How do you know it was Billy Harris?"

"When I ran outside, I saw the back of Billy's bike in the distance. He had just delivered my newspaper and was on his way to the next house down the road. Billy never did like Terrie. The other day I saw him kick her away from his bike. Terrie was just being friendly, weren't you, my darling lambkins?"

"I bet," muttered Dumpty under his breath. He didn't want Mrs. Smithers to file a complaint with his sergeant.

Officer Dumpty examined the fresh bike track in the dirt road in front of the Smithers's house. "I'll bring Billy back to the scene of the crime," he said.

A short time later, Billy pedaled up to the Smithers's house, Dumpty driving behind him. Terrie started growling at Billy, and Mrs. Smithers warned, "Keep away from my dog, you beast!"

Dumpty was reluctant to get out of his car while Terrie was unleashed, but a policeman must be brave. He stepped up to Billy and gazed sternly at the boy: "Did you throw stones at Mrs. Smithers's dog while delivering her paper?"

Billy looked scared. "No way," he said. "I like dogs."

Dumpty turned to Mrs. Smithers. "You didn't see Billy throw the stones. Could it have been anyone else?"

"Well ..." said the woman slowly. "No other bicycles have gone by, I'm sure. But I heard some noises outside just before the stone hit my front door. It sounded like kids laughing. It might have been one of them."

"It probably was," said Dumpty, who had been thinking furiously. He wanted to solve the case and get away from that vicious dog as quickly as possible. "Billy Harris never threw stones at your dog."

Examine the picture on the following page of Officer Dumpty speaking with Mrs. Smithers. How did he know it wasn't Billy who threw the stones?

FILE ENTRY: Voice Disguise

A detective sometimes needs to disguise his or her voice when speaking on the telephone. A good way to do this is to talk with a pencil between your teeth. (It takes practice to do it well!)

FILE ENTRY: Telephone Code

The numbers on your telephone can be used to send a secret code. Except for 1 and 0, there are three letters above each number. For example, 8 goes with the letters T, U, and V.

To write a note in telephone code, find each letter in your secret message on the phone diagram. Then write down the number instead. Put a small line above the number to show whether it is the first, middle, or last letter of the number. For example:

T would be written as 8\

U would be written as 8|

V would be written as 8/

Since there is no Q or Z on the phone, let the number 1 represent Q and the number 0 represent Z.

Here is how to encode the word DANGER

\ \ /\ \ | |
326437

Can you figure out this
secret message?

```
/ | \ /   \ / \ /   \ |   \ \ | / /     / / / / /   \ / | |   / |   | / | | / |
5387 7529 26 27745 36657 5653 66 266643
```

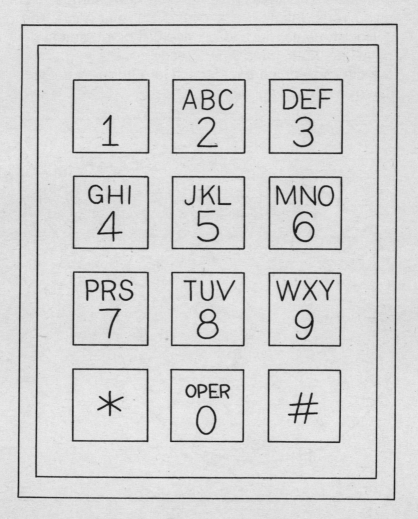

	ABC	DEF
1	2	3
GHI	JKL	MNO
4	5	6
PRS	TUV	WXY
7	8	9
*	OPER 0	#

FILE ENTRY: Making a Compass

If you are on a secret mission and get lost, you can make a compass by using your watch.

Hold the watch flat and point the hour hand in the direction of the sun. Then draw an imaginary line from the center of the watch midway between the number 12 and the hour hand. The line will point almost directly south.

Here is an example:

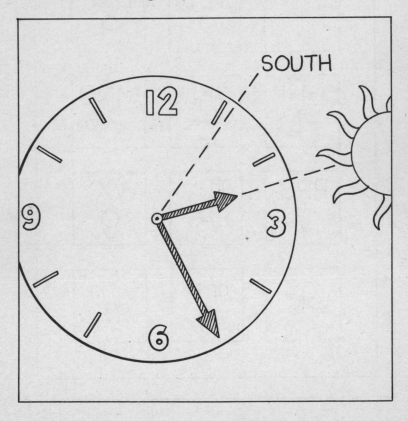

FILE ENTRY: Mystery Riddle

Ronald was running toward home. Suddenly, he saw a masked man. He quickly stopped, turned around, and began running back in the direction he had come from. Almost at once, though, he deliberately slid to the ground and stopped. **Why?**

DETECTIVE CASEFILE #6

The Case of the Unfortunate Fan

After signing off on his car radio, a famished Officer Fred Dumpty took one last bite of his sugar-glazed doughnut, turned on the siren (next to eating, he liked doing this best), and raced to Hargrove Auditorium. Jimmy Hansen was nervously pacing outside.

"You got here just in time," said Jimmy. "He's still hiding out in the parking lot."

The boy got into the car and Dumpty began cruising past rows of parked cars ... until it dawned on him that he didn't know who he was looking for — or why. It was a bad way to begin a case. "What happened, Jimmy?"

"Someone picked the wallet out of my back pocket while I was waiting to get into the concert. Gastric Juice is the most radical heavy metal band around, and now I'll never get to see them play." From what Dumpty had heard of this group, he thought Jimmy should feel fortunate. Gastric Juice couldn't compare with the rock 'n' roll he had enjoyed as a youngster.

Jimmy fought back tears. Dumpty tried to console him by mentioning how he had once missed the chance to see a Beatles concert. "Who are the Beatles?" asked Jimmy, wiping his eyes on his sleeve.

"Never mind," said Dumpty, suddenly feeling old. "Tell me your story."

"I was in the middle of the crowd, waiting for the main doors to open. Suddenly I felt something pulling at my back pocket. When I reached for my wallet, it was gone. Then I saw this guy behind me push his way out of the crowd. He was the one who took my wallet. It had twenty-five dollars in it and my concert ticket."

"Did you get a good look at him?" asked Dumpty.

"No, he was running toward the parking lot when I spotted him. He was wearing a red jacket and a baseball cap. I ran after the guy, but lost him. He must have ducked behind some cars."

Looking sadly out the patrol car window, Jimmy said, "I bought the ticket a month ago. Now I'm missing everything."

After an hour of cruising, Dumpty drove to the parking lot exit and turned off the motor. "There are so many places to hide, we'll never find him. Let's wait here. This is the only way out, and he'll have to pass by us. In the meantime, do you think you can run over to the concession stand and buy me a couple of hot dogs?"

When the concert ended, the front doors of the auditorium opened and people began pushing their way out, streaming past the two. While Officer Dumpty was finishing off his frankfurter, Jimmy grabbed his arm.

"Over there. There's someone wearing a red jacket and baseball cap."

Dumpty dabbed the mustard off his mouth, walked over to the man, and asked him his name. The man's hat was shoved down over his forehead. A pair of eyes squinted at Dumpty. "Brad Lathrop," he said. "What's the problem, Officer?"

"I'm looking for someone who stole a wallet. He's been hiding in the parking lot."

"Well, it wasn't me," said Lathrop. "I was watching the concert from a front row seat."

"Can you prove it?" asked Dumpty. "Did anyone you know see you there?"

"Nah, I was sitting next to strangers. But here is my ticket. It proves I was at the concert."

The man dug into his pocket and, with a smirk, handed a ticket to Officer Dumpty. The ticket was for the Gastric Juice concert, all right.

Dumpty turned to Jimmy. "Could this be yours?"

Jimmy shook his head. "I can't be sure. There were no seat numbers, just a ticket number. And I can't remember what my ticket number was."

The man in the red jacket looked relieved. "I told you that's my ticket," he said. "What a concert!

Gastric Juice sang all their big hits, like 'Everything Is Rotten.' " As Lathrop started to sing the song, Dumpty tuned him out and began thinking. Then he spoke.

"I think you're lying. You never bought a ticket to the concert. You came here just to rob someone. I'm taking you to police headquarters."

"Hey," shouted the man, "you've got nothing on me."

But Dumpty did.

Examine the picture on the following page of Dumpty speaking with the man in the red jacket. How did he know he had caught the pickpocket?

FILE ENTRY: Secret Line Messages

The drawing below has all the lines needed to make every letter of the alphabet. It can be used to send secret messages.

For some letters, you need to lift your pencil. Use a comma to indicate a new line. For example, the letter K is 68, 293.

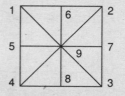

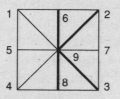

For example, if the first letter of your message is an N, the code would be 4132. To unscramble the code, place a piece of paper over the above diagram and draw a line from 4 to 1, from 1 to 3, and from 3 to 2. Your N will look like this:

Letters can be written more than one way. For example, the letter H could be written as 14, 57, 23; or 41, 95, 86 (as well as several other ways).

Can you figure out the word below?

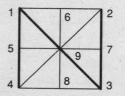

215734 1432 862793
41695   862793   68
437512 2157, 543

FILE ENTRY: Handwriting Analysis

Sometimes a detective can tell something about a person by studying his or her handwriting. Below are six messages.

Can you match each message (1–6) with the description (A–F) of the person who wrote it?

A. Was written by an Englishman
B. Was traced from someone else's note
C. Contains a hidden message

D. Was written by someone disguising his or her handwriting
E. Was written by a lefty
F. Was written in a hurry

1

7/16/88

Follow my directions to find the hidden money. First go to the rock by the oak tree. It is twelve paces to the rock.

2

7/16/88

Follow my dIrections to fiNd The Hidden monEy. First go To the Rock by thE oak tree. It is twelve paces to thE rock.

3   16/7/88

Follow my directions to find the hidden money. First go to the rock by the oak tree. It is twelve paces to the rock.

4   7/16/88

Follow my directions to find the hidden money. First go to the rock by the oak tree. It is twelve paces to the rock.

5   7/16/88

Follow my directions to find the hidden money. First go to the rock by the oak tree. It is twelve paces to the rock.

6   7/16/88

Follow my directions to find the hidden money. First go to the rock by the oak tree. It is twelve paces to the rock.

FILE ENTRY: Mystery Riddle

Frank Cummings worked for the Sunshine Bus Company for fourteen years. He was one of their most reliable drivers. One day a policeman saw Frank going the wrong way down a one-way street. But the officer didn't give Cummings a ticket. **Why?**

DETECTIVE CASEFILE #7

The
Case of the Bumbling
Burglar

Sundays were usually slow at police headquarters. Officer Fred Dumpty was at his desk munching a doughnut and puzzling over the Sunday crossword. He was just about to fill in the answer to 6 Down ("Italian pie" — PIZZA, one of his favorite foods), when the phone rang. "Great," Dumpty grumbled. "Just when I was about to write my first answer in one of these things."

"Hello, police? This is Greg Winters," whispered a voice. "Quick, send someone to 28 Skyline Drive. There's someone in my bedroom, I can hear. ..."

The voice faded away. Dumpty could hear a sharp crack as the phone receiver hit something — probably the floor. Then he heard the muted voice of Mr. Winters shouting. "Hey, drop that! The police are on the way, they'll find you!"

Dumpty scrambled to his patrol car. Yes, he thought as he drove toward Skyline Drive, the police are on the way. He enjoyed being a figure of law and order, and prided himself on his perfect crime-solving record.

When Dumpty arrived at the Winters's house, the front door was locked. At the rear of the house he found a concrete patio, and behind it a large wooded area. The back door was open. Preparing himself for the worst, Dumpty pulled out his revolver.

"I'm over here," shouted a voice behind him. Dumpty swung around and saw a man stumbling out of the woods. He was wearing a bathrobe and slippers. The slippers were covered with bits of wood and brambles.

"I'm Greg Winters," the man panted. "I'm afraid I lost him. He ran off toward the highway."

"Tell me what happened here," said Dumpty as he holstered his gun.

"I was reading in my den," said Winters, "when I heard funny noises. At first I thought it was kids playing in the street, but then I heard drawers opening and closing in my bedroom." Winters gestured toward the other end of the house. "That's when I called the police. Was it you I spoke to?"

Officer Dumpty nodded and glanced at the man's feet. Winters's slippers had rabbit faces on them. "What were you doing in the woods?" he asked.

"When I was on the phone with you," Winters explained, "I saw a man run into the woods. I dropped the phone and ran after him. I can usually run pretty fast, but these slippers held me back."

"Can you describe the man?" asked Dumpty.

"Well, he was wearing jeans and a gray sweatshirt, and he had brown hair. But I only saw him from the back. I'm afraid it's not much help."

Dumpty looked at Greg's worried face. "We'd better go inside and see if anything is missing."

"I heard the guy go into my closet," said Greg. "I keep my coin collection in there. I hope he didn't steal it. It's worth a lot of money." He added, "At least I'm insured."

Dumpty took off his hat and scratched his head. He wanted to wrap up the case quickly, because he was getting hungry again. "You know, Mr. Winters, I'll bet your coin collection *is* missing. But it wasn't stolen. I think you made up this story so that you could collect the insurance money."

Examine the picture of Officer Dumpty talking to Greg Winters. Why did Dumpty suspect that the robbery was a fake?

FILE ENTRY: Questioning the Suspect

Asking the right questions can help a detective solve a crime or catch a criminal. Here are three suspects. After reading the facts, what *one* question would tell you whether or not the suspect was guilty?

SUSPECT #1

You board a train in search of a criminal, whom you suspect is on the train and heading for Greenville, fifty miles away. You believe he plans to flee the country from the Greenville airport. A man who looks like your suspect is reading a newspaper in the last car. The conductor tells you the man has no identification but claims to be going to Greenville for some shopping and plans to return that evening. **What do you ask the suspect?**

FILE ENTRY: Questioning the Suspect

SUSPECT #2

You trail a spy to a small farm village. You suspect he arrived that morning and is disguised as a farmer. You see a man who is hoeing a field and is dressed like a farmer. His dungarees are dirty. Beads of perspiration dot his forehead. He seems nervous as you approach him. **What do you ask him?**

FILE ENTRY: Questioning the Suspect

You arrive at a mansion where there has been a burglary. The owner claims he found a window open and a valuable antique statue missing from the hallway. His dog, Brutus, sniffs the carpet where the statue once stood. The owner suspects his servant committed the robbery, but the burglar could have been a stranger. **What do you ask the owner?**

FILE ENTRY: Under Surveillance

Sometimes a detective must watch a suspect without the person knowing he or she is being observed. You can pretend to be reading a magazine while still keeping your suspect under surveillance. Here's how:

Cut out a small circle from the front pages of an open magazine. Then, tape a small mirror on the opposite page.

Pretend to be reading the magazine. If your suspect is in front of you, watch him or her through the peephole. If he or she is behind you, hold the magazine so you can see him or her in the mirror.

HOLE   MIRROR

FILE ENTRY: Mystery Riddle

Officer Franklin responded to a police call. A woman was sitting on a tenth-floor windowsill and threatening to jump. There were no awnings or ledges to break her fall to the concrete pavement below. As Franklin got out of his police car, she suddenly fell off the sill. But she wasn't hurt. **What happened?**

DETECTIVE CASEFILE #8

The Case of the Down-and-Out Delivery Man

Officer Fred Dumpty was taking a beating. The man he was fighting swung his fist and hit Dumpty square in the nose. Dumpty went down in a heap.

"Are you all right?" asked his opponent, rookie cop Steve Porter.

The two men were boxing in the makeshift ring in the basement of police headquarters; the cops used it to keep in shape. Dumpty staggered to his feet and sat up against the ropes. "I guess I'm no Mike Tyson," he laughed, removing his boxing gloves.

"You're not even a Pee-wee Herman," replied Porter. Dumpty was too sore to answer the cocky young cop.

The next day, because he was so bruised, Dumpty was given duty at the front desk of the police station. Nothing much happened until that afternoon, when a young man lurched through the front door.

Dumpty recognized him. It was Dennis Bean, the delivery man who worked at Walter's Drugstore.

Dennis looked faint; his face was bruised and his lip was slightly swollen. Dumpty helped him to a chair and handed him an ice bag. "Tell me what happened," said Dumpty.

"Around two o'clock every afternoon, Mr. Walter has me take the money from the cash register over to Middle Land Bank. Today, while I was driving down Market Street, I saw a man on a motorcycle parked by the side of the road. He flagged me down.

"I stopped my truck to help him. The money was in a bag on the front seat next to me. When I opened the door and got out, he rushed over, grabbed my shoulder with one hand, and pinned me against the side of my truck."

Dennis took out a handkerchief and blew his nose hard.

"Then he punched me right in the face. I slid down to the ground. I must have blacked out for a minute. When I woke up, the money was gone."

Just at that moment, Officer Steve Porter walked

by the two men. "Hey," he said to Dennis, chuckling, "I know Dumpty didn't hit you. His punch wouldn't hurt a flea."

Ignoring Porter, Dumpty grabbed a pencil and a police form. The sudden movement made his badly bruised nose throb. "I'll need a description for our patrol cars. What did he look like?"

Dennis thought for a minute. "He had on a motorcycle helmet so I couldn't make out his face. But he was tall. Maybe six feet or more, and real strong. Like this guy here." He pointed at Porter.

"Anything else?" asked Dumpty.

Dennis shook his head. "I can't remember. It all happened too fast. But I do remember the muscles bulging out of his black T-shirt."

Dumpty looked at Dennis Bean's battered face. "So he knocked you out with just one punch?"

"He must have been a professional fighter or something," said Dennis. "He just wound up and slugged me. One punch and I was out."

Officer Porter, who was still listening, said, "This motorcycle guy sounds like he might give me a good fight — or at least a better one than Fred gave me yesterday."

Battling the urge to hurl it at Porter, Officer Dumpty put down his pencil. His throbbing nose made concentrating difficult — but it also helped him sort out the problem. He gave a disdainful glance at Porter, then stared hard at Dennis Bean.

"Where did you hide the money?"

Dennis straightened up and grabbed the sides of his chair. "What do you mean?"

"There was no man on a motorcycle," said Dumpty.

"Why don't you tell me what really happened before you get into deeper trouble?"

Officer Porter looked at Dumpty with his mouth open in astonishment.

Examine the picture of Officer Dumpty questioning Dennis Bean. How did he know the delivery man had faked the robbery?

FILE ENTRY: Shopping List Code

A good way to hide a secret message is to make it look like a shopping list.

The number in front of each item tells your friend, who will read the message, the number of letters to count. For example, the letter A could be coded as "5 pizzas," since A is the fifth letter in the word PIZZAS. If there is no number next to an item, the first letter of the word should be used.

The shopping list below encodes the message HOORAY:

2 cheese
2 sodas
orange juice
4 pears
2 cat food
yogurt

Now can you find the secret message in this shopping list?

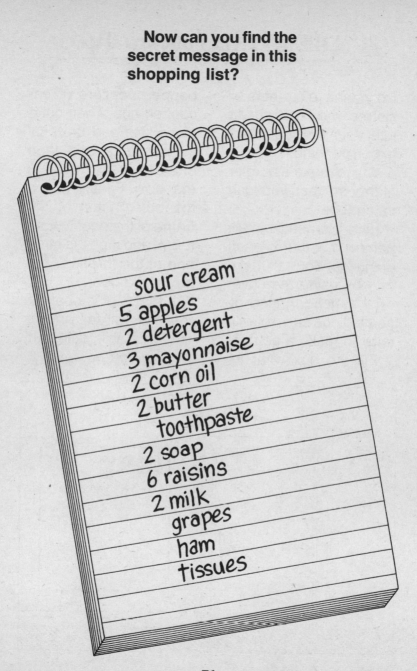

sour cream
5 apples
2 detergent
3 mayonnaise
2 corn oil
2 butter
toothpaste
2 soap
6 raisins
2 milk
grapes
ham
tissues

FILE ENTRY: Popcorn Tip

Do you have brothers or sisters who like to sneak into your room at night to borrow things? Here's a way to make a burglar alarm so that you can catch them.

First, you need a small, narrow box that is open at the top. You can make one by using the cover of a matchbox, and by sealing one end of it with tape to make a bottom.

Fill the box with un- popped popcorn or un- cooked rice. Then cut a piece of thread about six inches long, and tape one end of the thread to the box. Finally, place the box on top of the frame of the door to your room, and tape the other end of the thread to the top of the door.

If the door is opened, the box will fall and its contents will spill out, waking you up.

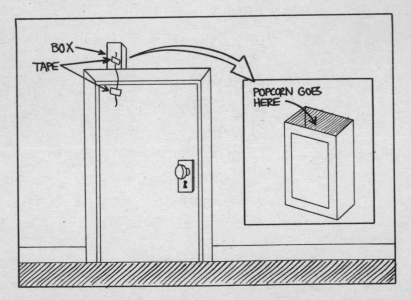

FILE ENTRY: Mystery Riddle

A policeman arrested two girls for spraying paint on a stop sign. The girls looked exactly alike. They were born on the same day in the same year and they had the same parents. But the girls were not twins. **How could this be?**

The
Case of the Diner
Disasters

Cruising through town early one morning, Officer Fred Dumpty felt grumpy. He was on a diet. For breakfast, Dumpty usually ate bacon and pancakes with plenty of syrup, a glass of milk, sausages, buttered toast, some orange juice, and a corn muffin. All he had had today was cereal with skim milk. "I ate fifteen minutes ago and I'm hungry already. I'm never going to make it to lunch." Though he didn't do it on purpose, Dumpty soon found himself driving down Maple Street, toward an area of town that had a lot of restaurants. None of the restaurants was open yet, and the sidewalks were empty.

As he passed Pulski's Restaurant, Dumpty noticed something strange and stopped the car. Outside the locked front door of Pulski's was stacked the morning's bakery delivery. Dumpty observed that several pies and cakes had been removed from their boxes, and that someone had taken big bites out of them. A large brown paper bag full of dinner rolls had been ripped apart and scattered across the pavement. On the sidewalk was a squashed lemon meringue pie. Imagine ruining all this good food, Dumpty thought sadly. He grabbed his radio mike. "There's been some vandalism and theft at Pulski's. Better tell Mr. Pulski to come over quickly."

About ten minutes later, the store owner arrived. "What a catastrophe!" he shouted. "Whoever did this should go to jail."

"Calm down, Mr. Pulski," said Dumpty. "I'm on the job, so you can be confident the case will be solved."

That statement did not seem to put Mr. Pulski's mind at ease. "This is the third incident this week," said the unhappy owner. "Monday someone squirted ketchup across the front window. Tuesday we kept getting take-out orders over the phone for addresses that didn't exist. And now today, this."

Dumpty bent down and examined the squashed lemon meringue pie. A bicycle had ridden over it. One of its tires had left a short trail.

"I'll bet it's those Thomas kids," muttered Mr. Pulski. "I chased them away from the front of my restaurant a few days ago, but they kept riding by with their bikes and making noise, and they almost knocked down one of my customers." Mr. Pulski pointed in the direction of the tire track: "See. They live in that direction, a few miles down. Hey, Dumpty, you can get your nose out of the pie now and check on the kids. C'mon, Dumpty, I'll give you a piece of cake if you're that hungry."

"No thanks," sighed the policeman, getting up, "I'm on a diet."

It wasn't long before Dumpty pulled up to the Thomas house. As he got out of the car, he heard noises coming from the open garage. There were Tim and Kim huddled over a bicycle.

"Where have you kids been for the last hour?" asked Dumpty. Tim nudged his sister with his elbow. Kim straightened up. "We've been cleaning my bike."

"Yeah," said Tim, "we've been cleaning her bike. Is that against the law?"

"Someone broke into bags of food in front of a restaurant on Maple Street," said Dumpty sternly. "Let me have a look at those tires."

"It wasn't us," said Tim. "We haven't been near Pulski's since Monday."

Dumpty examined the front and back whitewall tires. The rear tire looked as if it had just been washed. It was still wet.

"How come you kids cleaned off just one of the tires?"

"Uhh, we were just about to do the front," said Tim.

"Uhh, we ran out of soap," said Kim at the same instant.

"Well, I think both of you are lying," said Dumpty. "You were the ones who vandalized Pulski's Restaurant. And you cleaned the rear tire because it was covered with lemon meringue."

Examine the picture on the following page of Officer Dumpty in front of Pulski's Restaurant. How did he know the Thomas kids were lying??

FILE ENTRY: Clue Search

When a detective searches for tiny clues (or when he or she searches for a lost object), it is important to see that none of the areas is skipped over. Here's how to do a really thorough search.

Inside a house or building, divide the rooms into areas. Then slowly examine each.

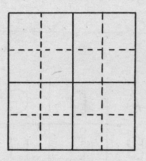

Outside a house, divide the area into a grid (stretch string or use wooden stakes). Then move through the grid as shown by the dotted line.

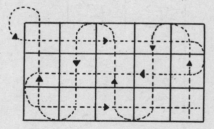

To search a very large area, use an ever-widening circle. Start at the center and work outward in a spiral.

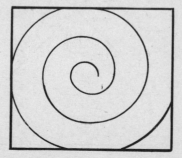

FILE ENTRY: Pigpen Code

These diagrams are the key to a secret alphabet code you can use to send a hidden message. It's called a "pig-pen code" because each letter is in a compartment, or pen, that has a unique shape.

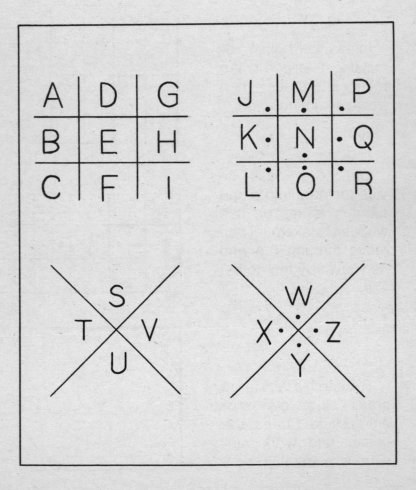

To send your message, draw the outline of the compartment each letter is in, including a dot if there is one. For example, here is how to send the message "WATCH OUT":

**Can you decipher
this secret message?**

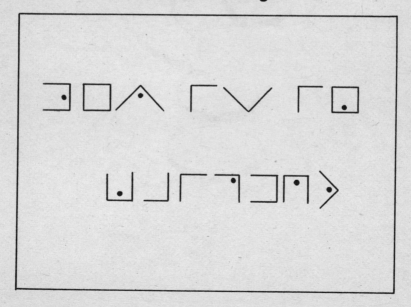

FILE ENTRY: Mystery Riddle

Officer Neale chased a robber who was escaping in a getaway car. The policeman managed to overtake him, even though his squad car had a flat tire. **How could this be?**

DETECTIVE CASEFILE #10

The Case of the Stolen Exam

Officer Fred Dumpty was going through some very old math tests he had taken as a student. "I don't know why I kept these," he said to himself. "Mr.

Erwin always took off points because of food stains and crumbs on the paper. But who could get through an hour-long exam without *some* refreshment?"

Just then the phone rang. "Hello, Fredrick? This is Erwin at the Washington School." What a coincidence, thought Dumpty. "I hate to bother you but I have a problem and could use your help."

"Of course, Mr. Erwin. What is it?" Dumpty asked.

"Someone got into my desk, Fredrick, and stole the answers to the final exam. It just happened — I was only out of my office a couple of minutes. I need to find the thief quickly or I'll have to write a new exam for the kids to take during their vacation. You remember how boring summer school is, don't you, Fredrick?"

Dumpty checked his watch. It was four-thirty. "Are any children still in the school?" he asked.

"Only Ms. Fernandez's students. They're having a dress rehearsal for a play."

"Okay. Keep everyone there. I'll be right over. And please don't call me Fredrick."

Within ten minutes, Officer Dumpty was knocking on Mr. Erwin's office door. He fought back the painful memories of math class.

"Hello, Fredrick!" (He pronounced it "Fred-er-rick.") "Glad you're here. Now, the answers were in the top drawer of my desk, here."

Dumpty examined the room. Noticing a glass on one of the file cabinets, he asked, "Is this your glass of orange juice, Mr. Erwin?"

The teacher's face brightened. "No, it must have been left by the person who stole the answers."

With his fingertips, Dumpty picked up the glass by

its edge and held it up to the light, studying it carefully.

"This glass has no fingerprints," said Dumpty. He paused to think for a moment. "Does anyone in the play have a costume with gloves?"

"Good thinking, Fredrick! I'll run over to the auditorium and check."

A few minutes later, Mr. Erwin returned with two children, one dressed as a dog, the other as a queen.

"Take off your masks," said Dumpty, "and tell me your names."

The queen lifted her bulky crown off her head and said, "Thank you, we've been wearing these things all afternoon. My name is Kelly."

The dog had been struggling to get his mask off and finally did so with Mr. Erwin's help. "I'm Tony," he said. "Why did you bring us here?"

"Well," Dumpty explained, "some test papers were stolen from Mr. Erwin's desk. We found a glass here with no fingerprints on it, so we figured the thief might have had gloves on. Tony, is this your glass?"

"No, sir. See, I've got my own glass." Tony held up a glass of juice.

"But why is your glass almost full?" asked Dumpty. "Kelly said you had been rehearsing for a while."

"I, uh, I finished one glass already. This is my second. I was just drinking it when Mr. Erwin fetched me from the auditorium."

Dumpty turned to Kelly. "Then is this *your* glass, Kelly?"

"No, it's not. This is the only glass I've had." She held up an almost empty glass of juice.

Dumpty nodded and solemnly walked over to Tony.

85

"Why don't you give the answer sheets back to your teacher, Tony. You're in enough trouble already."

Examine the picture of Dumpty with Tony and Kelly. How did he know the boy had taken the answers?

FILE ENTRY: Police Lineup

It was almost midnight when Frank O'Neill flagged down a police car on the main highway. He could barely speak as he told the policeman that he had been attacked on a country road about a half mile away. His watch and wallet had been stolen. It was dark and he could not see his attacker.

O'Neill said that when he tried to get away, the robber grabbed his shoulder with one hand and punched him in the face with the other. From his picture above, you can see the injury was not very serious.

A police search located five persons in the area who were unable to produce an alibi for the time of the attack. They are pictured in the police lineup at right.

Can you pick out the robber?

FILE ENTRY: Deck-of-Cards Code

You can send a secret message to a friend using an old deck of cards. The cards should have a picture on the backs. Arrange the cards so all the pictures are turned in the same direction.

Separate the cards into suits. Then, for each suit, put the cards in order from ace to king. Now, stack the cards with the ace of spades on the top, followed by all the hearts, all the diamonds, and all the clubs.

You are ready to write your secret message. Square the deck neatly and hold the cards tightly together. With a pencil, print your secret mes-

sage around the sides of the deck.

To hide your message, all you have to do is mix up the cards. Turn the top half of the deck around so the pictures on the backs face in the opposite direction. Then shuffle the two halves together and your message will completely vanish.

When your friend gets the deck, he or she arranges the backs so they all face one way. Then he or she places the cards in the order you originally had them.

Your secret message will reappear around the edges!

FILE ENTRY: Mystery Riddle

When Officer Wallace patrolled his beat, it took him one hour and twenty minutes to walk one way. Without walking any faster, it took him only eighty minutes to return. **How come?**

DETECTIVE CASEFILE #1
THE CASE OF THE SOGGY SUSPECT

The picture shows that the man's jacket is dripping wet. This means he must have been outside during the rainstorm. Since it began raining just as Mrs. Turner's purse was stolen, the man could not have been in the restaurant for an hour, as he said he was.

Footprint Clues
1. B (running)
2. E (limping)
3. D (pushing a wheelbarrow)
4. A (pulling a wagon)
5. C (very tall person walking; notice the long strides, which would be made by someone with long legs)
6. F (walking with a cane)

Ruler Code
Wait for me.

DETECTIVE CASEFILE #2
THE CASE OF THE BALD-HEADED SUSPECT

Dumpty suddenly remembered that one of the items the shopper bought was a comb. The stranger couldn't have been the escaped criminal. Bart Hargrove was completely bald, and would have no reason to buy a comb. It seems that Dumpty did pay attention to appearances after all.

Lip Reading
1. E
2. A
3. F
4. D
5. B
6. C

Mystery Riddle
They crawled through the sewer pipe at different times.

DETECTIVE CASEFILE #3
THE CASE OF THE
SNOWBALL SLINGER

If Mrs. Hummer arrived home after Tommy, her coat would be hanging on top of his. But the picture shows that Tommy's coat is on top of his mother's. Therefore, he must have arrived home later in the afternoon than his mother.

Secret Graph Code
Meet me in the park after school.

Mystery Riddle
Henry was a police dog.

DETECTIVE CASEFILE #4 THE CASE OF THE LOST LOCOMOTIVE

Nancy Gibson said she was looking through a magazine with the clubhouse door open. But the melted wax was on the front of the candle. If Nancy had been reading by candlelight, the breeze would have caused the dripped wax to spill down the other side of the candle—away from the door. Sherlock Holmes would have been proud of Dumpty.

Spotting Spots
A. 2
B. 6 (From higher up, the drop makes a harder splash.)
C. 3
D. 4
E. 1
F. 5 (This spot is running down the wall, while all the others are on the floor.)

Mystery Riddle
The police officers were facing each other.

DETECTIVE CASEFILE #5
THE CASE OF THE DARLING DOG

If Billy had thrown both the newspaper and the stones from his bicycle, he would have had to slow down to do it. Then the tire from his bike would have made a wobbly line as he tried to keep his balance, like the line leading up to his bike in the picture. But the track that Billy's bike made earlier, when he delivered the paper, is straight.

Telephone Code
Let's play an April Fool's joke on Bonnie.

Mystery Riddle
Ronald was in a baseball game. He was running from third base to home and was met by the catcher, who was wearing a catcher's mask. He stopped, ran back to third, and slid in to avoid being tagged.

The man showed Dumpty a whole concert ticket, not the stub. If he had entered the auditorium, the ticket-taker would have torn the ticket in half. Therefore, Dumpty knew the man was lying.

Secret Line Messages
Surprise

Handwriting Analysis
A. 3 (The date is written with the day, month, and year, in that order.)
B. 5 (While the message was being traced, the top paper was shifted, and part of the second and third lines are at an angle.)
C. 2 (Look for the capital letters in the sentences. The message says "IN THE TREE.")
D. 6 (The capital F beginning the first sentence is different from the one beginning the second sentence, showing that the writer tried to disguise his handwriting but forgot to change an F.)
E. 4 (Note the left-handed slant of the letters.)
F. 1 (See how a letter is scratched out, a punctuation mark is missing, and a *t* is not crossed.)

Mystery Riddle
Frank Cummings happened to be walking home after a hard day's work.

98

DETECTIVE CASEFILE #7
THE CASE OF THE
BUMBLING BURGLAR

Through the window, Dumpty saw the receiver resting on the telephone cradle.

But he had heard the receiver fall to the floor as Winters supposedly ran after the thief. Caught by his mistake, Winters admitted setting up the robbery.

Questioning the Suspect
1. *Where is your train ticket?* If the passenger were a fleeing criminal, he would have a one-way ticket.
2. *May I see your hands?*
If the man's hands are not heavily calloused, chances are he's not a farmer.
3. *Did the dog bark?*
If not, the robber must have been someone the dog knew—possibly the servant.

Mystery Riddle
The woman fell backward and landed inside the room.

DETECTIVE CASEFILE #8
THE CASE OF THE DOWN-
AND-OUT DELIVERY MAN

Dennis claimed that he was knocked down with only one punch. But if this were true, both his cheeks would not have been bruised unless a very large fist hit him right in the middle of his face. But since the picture shows that Dennis's nose was un-harmed, he had to be lying. Dennis soon admitted that he had faked the robbery and stolen the money himself.

Shopping List Code
See you tonight.

Mystery Riddle
The two girls had another sister. They were triplets.

DETECTIVE CASEFILE #9
THE CASE OF THE DINER DISASTERS

The picture shows that there were at least three restaurants on Maple Street. Officer Dumpty never told the twins which restaurant's food had been ruined. The only way Tim and Kim could have known it was Pulski's was if they had been there that morning. Once Officer Dumpty pointed this out, Tim and Kim admitted their guilt.

Pigpen Code
Key is in mailbox.

Mystery Riddle
The tire that was flat was the spare one in the squad car's trunk.

DETECTIVE CASEFILE #10
THE CASE OF THE STOLEN EXAM

With his mask on, it was impossible for Tony to drink from the juice glass he was holding because it had no straw. The mouth of the mask was too small. Tony needed a glass with a straw—the one he had left on the file cabinet.

Police Lineup
Suspect #2 is the guilty person. The gash on O'Neill's right cheek shows the robber used his left hand to punch him. The gash was made by a jeweled ring. Suspect #2 is the only person wearing a ring on his left hand.

Mystery Riddle
It took officer Wallace the same amount of time each way. One hour and twenty minutes is the same as eighty minutes.